THIS BOOK
BELONGS TO

SBN 361 00499 0

Published by Purnell Books, Paulton, Bristol,
BS18 5LQ, a member of the BPCC group of companies.
Reprinted 1983
Made and printed in Great Britain by Purnell and Sons
(Book Production) Ltd, Paulton, Bristol.

NODDY
AND THE BUMPY-DOG

BY
Enid Blyton

CONTENTS

LONDON
SAMPSON LOW, MARSTON & CO., LTD.
AND RICHARDS PRESS LTD.

© Enid Blyton
as to the text herein and
Sampson Low, Marston & Co. Ltd.
as to the artwork herein 1957

NODDY SANG A LITTLE SONG TO MISS RABBIT AND
MISS BEAR BECAUSE HE FELT SO HAPPY.

1. ICE-CREAMS FOR THREE

"COME along, little car," said Noddy, getting into it. "We'll go and see if we can find any-one who wants to be taken to the station. You do look nice and shiny this morning."

"Parp-parp!" said the car, sounding very pleased, and out into the road they went. Noddy waved to Mrs. Tubby Bear next door and she waved back.

"There goes little Noddy," she said to Mr. Tubby Bear, who was digging his garden, ready to plant his seeds. "What a hard-working little fellow he is, to be sure!"

Noddy had quite a busy morning. First he

took Mr. Noah to the station to meet Mrs. Noah, who had been to stay with her aunt. Then he took Miss Toy Rabbit to the market to buy herself a pink ribbon to match her frock.

"Come and help me to buy one, Noddy," said Miss Rabbit, who was really very sweet. But Noddy didn't think he could choose ribbons.

"Look," he said, "there's little Tessie Bear over there. *She* will help you! Tessie, Tessie! Hallo!"

Little Tessie Bear came hurrying up. She smiled at Little Noddy, and kissed Miss Toy Rabbit, who lived in the same street as she did.

"You look very nice today, Tessie Bear," said Noddy. "I do like that little blue bow under your chin. Look—can you choose some ribbons with Miss Toy Rabbit? Then I'll take you both to have an ice-cream."

So Tessie Bear went to buy ribbons with Miss Rabbit, and Noddy waited in his car for them. Mr. Wobbly Man came by and said good morning.

Katie Kangaroo came jumping up.

"Do you want me to carry any shopping for you in my pocket?" she said.

"No, thank you. I'm not shopping this morning," said Noddy. "Anyway, your pouch looks pretty full already."

"Yes. Mrs. Noah went to visit her aunt, so I've been doing her shopping," said Katie Kangaroo.

9

"Well, goodbye—I must get back to the Ark."

Away she jumped, leaping right over a lamp-post as she went. "Goodness— what a way to get along!" said Noddy. "She's a *very* jumpy person. Oh—here comes little Tessie Bear and Miss Rabbit. Come along, you two. Jump into my car and we'll go and have some ice-creams."

"Are you sure you can afford to buy ice-creams for three people?" said Tessie Bear, sitting next to Noddy. "Oh, Miss Rabbit—have I left you enough room."

"Oh yes. It's a bit of a squeeze—but it *is* so nice to have a ride in a car," said Miss Rabbit. "I hardly ever do. Oooh—here's the ice-cream shop already. What a pity! I wish it was miles away!"

"Well, I'll take you to the one in Toy-Dog Town if you like," said Noddy, kindly. "That's a nice long ride, and the ice-cream shop is lovely there. But I hope you don't mind dogs."

"I love them," said Tessie Bear. But Miss Rabbit looked rather frightened.

"They won't chase me, will they?" she said. "You'll look after me, Little Noddy, won't you?"

"I'll look after you *both*," said Noddy, and off they went. Noddy sang a song because he felt so happy.

> "Oh little Miss Rabbit
> And little Miss Bear
> I really do think
> They're a nice little pair.
> I do love their noses,
> I do love their ears,
> It *is* fun to have them,
> They really are DEARS!"

"Oh NODDY! Did you make that song up just this very minute?" said Miss Rabbit, opening her big eyes very wide indeed. "Tessie Bear, isn't he clever?"

"Yes, very clever," said Tessie. "And kind too. He's quite the nicest person in Toy Village."

"Ooooh!" said Noddy, so pleased and surprised that he almost ran into a lamp-post. "Oooh, Tessie—nobody's ever said that to me before."

"Parp-parp!" said the car, just as pleased as Noddy, and gave a little hop, skip and jump.

"Behave yourself, car," said Noddy in surprise. "Miss Rabbit and Miss Bear won't like *you* if you tip them out! Ah—here's Toy-Dog Town —and there's the ice-cream shop."

Soon they were all having ice-creams in the

little shop. They were very, very big ones.

"You see, Toy Dogs have very large appetites," said Noddy. "They don't eat like us—they gulp! So if ever you want *large* ice-creams, go to Toy-Dog Town!"

They had just finished their ice-creams when something made them jump. It was a loud noise from outside the little shop. First a CRASH— and then barks and shouts.

"Wuff-wuff-wuff! Oooh, wuff-wuff-wuff!"

"You shouldn't have got in my way! It was *your* fault!"

"Oooh-wuff-oooh-wuff-oooh-wuff!"

"Don't make such a fuss! You're not hurt. Silly dog!"

Noddy ran to the door of the shop. Whatever could have happened?

2. THE POOR TOY DOG

A TOY dog lay in the road, barking—nearby was a bicycle lying on its side. A sailor doll was just picking himself up, looking very angry.

"Running across the road like that just as I was coming at top speed!" he said, picking up his hat and dusting it. "Look at my hat—all bent. I've a good mind to come and smack you."

"Wuff-wuff," said the dog, very sadly, and held up his front paw as if it hurt him. He got up and tried to run but he couldn't. He could only limp along on three legs. "Wuff," he said, and flopped down again.

"It serves you right," said the sailor doll. "Perhaps you won't run in front of bicycles another time. And don't think I'm going to bother about your paw, because I'm not!"

Then he got on his bicycle and away he went at top speed again.

"Oh!" said Noddy, quite shocked at such unkindness. "What a horrid fellow! You poor little dog—are you very much hurt?"

The dog limped over to Noddy, whining, holding up his paw. Tessie Bear stroked his head and Miss Rabbit patted him.

"I'll bandage your paw for you," said Noddy,

taking out his nice clean handkerchief. "Hold it up. There—that's right. I expect it's very bruised. You keep that bandage on for a day or two and your paw will soon heal."

"And *don't* bite it off," said Tessie Bear. "You're rather a nice dog. Have you got a name?"

"Wuff-wuff-wuff," said the dog, his head on one side, and his ears pricked up.

"I wonder if he belongs to anyone," said Miss Rabbit. "If he does, they'll look after him. Well, goodbye, dog. I hope your paw soon gets better."

The dog rubbed himself against her almost as if he were a cat, nearly knocking little Miss Rabbit over.

"Don't do that, dog," said Noddy. "Oh

goodness—now you've smacked Tessie Bear with that big waggy tail of yours. You needn't be *quite* so grateful to us. Oooh—now you've smacked *me* with your waggy tail."

"Run away home!" said Tessie Bear. "Go on, dog, run away home! Find your master. Home, dog, home!"

"Wuff!" said the dog, prancing round on three legs as if he wanted a game. "Wuff!"

"Let's get into the car," said Noddy. "He'll knock us *all* over if we stay any longer. He's a very very nice dog, but awfully bouncy and jumpy. Goodbye, dog!"

The dog whined loudly. He ran to the car and licked Noddy's hand. Then he ran round the other side to lick Tessie Bear and Miss Rabbit.

"Oh dear—he's made my hand so wet!" said Noddy. "Where's my hanky? I must dry it."

He felt in his pockets first one side and then another, but he *couldn't* find his hanky.

17

"I must have left it in the ice-cream shop," he said. "Oh dear—what a nuisance."

Tessie Bear gave a little giggle. "*I* know where it is," she said. "I can see it!"

"Where?" said Noddy, looking all round. "You *can't* see it, Tessie. Unless it's on top of my hat! That's the only place I can't see!"

Miss Rabbit gave a little giggle too. Then they both pointed to the dog, which was still prancing round the car on three legs.

"You tied up his poor leg with your hanky!" said Tessie, with a little squeal of laughter. "Oh Noddy, look, there it is!"

"Dear me—of course I did," said Noddy. "I ought to do what Big-Ears is always telling me to do—grow a few brains!"

"Goodbye, dog!" cried Miss Rabbit as the car drove off. "Take care of that paw!"

And away they went to Toy Village again. "I don't expect we shall ever see that dog again —*or* my hanky," said Noddy.

But he was quite wrong —they *did* see him.

18

3. A TALK WITH BIG-EARS

NODDY drove to Toy Village and Miss Rabbit and Tessie Bear both got out. "Thank you, Noddy," they said. "We *did* enjoy the ride and the ice-creams!"

"So did I," said Noddy. "Now I'm going to see Big-Ears and tell him about that poor dog."

And away he went through the wood to Big-Ears' toadstool house. Big-Ears was doing his washing, and he was very pleased to see Noddy.

"You've come just in time," he said. "Go and hang up these things on my line to dry, Noddy, will you?"

"I came to tell you about a poor dog," said Noddy, taking up a big pile of washed curtains. "Oooh—these *are* heavy, Big-Ears."

"Only because they are wet," said Big-Ears. "What's this about a poor dog? Hasn't he got any money?"

"I don't mean that kind of poor," said Noddy, struggling out of doors with the curtains. "Where are your pegs, Big-Ears?"

"In the peg-bag," said Big-Ears. "I'll bring it out with me." So he went out with Noddy, carrying the peg-bag and some more washing.

"How do you hang such big wet curtains on the line on such a windy day and peg them on at the same time?" said Noddy. "As soon as I let go the curtains to go to the peg-bag for a peg,

 they try to get away. Stop it, curtain—now you're flapping me in the face!"

"Oh Noddy—look, do as I do, and take some pegs and hold them in your mouth while you hang up

"HOLD SOME PEGS IN YOUR MOUTH WHILE YOU
HANG UP THE CURTAINS," SAID BIG-EARS.

21

the curtains—then peg them quickly," said Big-Ears. So Noddy took quite a lot of pegs and held them between his front teeth, while he struggled with an extra-big curtain.

"Now tell me about this dog," said Big-Ears, pegging away fast.

"Ee-woo-ee-gog-gog-woo-woo," said Noddy. Big-Ears looked round in surprise.

"What's that? Are you talking dog language, Noddy? I can't understand a word."

"Woo-gog-gog-eg-eg," said Noddy, his mouth full of pegs. Big-Ears began to laugh.

"Oh! You're holding the pegs in your mouth, of course. Mind you don't swallow one!"

"Ee-woo-ee-egg-egg-woo," mumbled Noddy, trying to hang the curtain straight on the line. The wind took hold of it and it blew off the line right on top of Noddy. He found himself on the

ground in complete darkness, with the curtain over him.

"Woo-eee-ogg-eg-wog-oo!" he cried, and Big-Ears began to laugh. He lifted the curtain off Noddy.

"I think I've swallowed a peg," said Noddy, alarmed. "I spat them all out when the curtain flapped on top of me—but I'm sure I had four in my mouth—and look, now there are only three! Oh, Big-Ears—does it matter swallowing a peg?"

"You'd have choked if you did," said Big-Ears. "Leave my washing alone now, Noddy. That curtain has gone into the mud—and I've a good mind to make you wash it all out for me again."

"Oh *no*," said Noddy, hurrying to his car. "No —I don't feel like washing this morning, Big-Ears.

Oh goodness me—what's this on my face?"

"Mud," said Big-Ears. "Where's your hanky?"

"I'll get it," said Noddy, and felt in his pockets.

"There now—you've come out without a hanky again," said Big-Ears, quite cross. "Haven't I told you you must ALWAYS have a hanky to cough and sneeze in! It's bad manners not to have a hanky, and . . ."

"Oh! I know! I remember now," said Noddy.

"I bandaged that dog's leg with it. Of course!"

"What dog's leg?" asked Big-Ears, pegging up a cushion cover. "For goodness' sake tell me about this dog."

"Well, I haven't had a *chance* yet!" said

Noddy. "Oh dear—my face *does* feel muddy."
He picked up a piece of cloth from the grass and
rubbed it over his face.

"Hey! That's a clean duster I've just washed!"
said Big-Ears, looking so cross that Noddy jumped
into his car at once and drove away.

"What about that DOG?" yelled Big-Ears.

"Tell you another time, when you're not so
busy!" shouted back Noddy. "Shoo, you rabbit—
get out of the way!"

4. NODDY HAS A BUSY DAY

NOW two days later, just as Noddy was cleaning his little car, ready to go out, someone
came running in at his front gate.

"Wuff!" said the Someone and jumped up at
Noddy's back. Noddy fell over at once.

"Oooh—what's that? Oh, it's *you*, dog. Well,
don't knock me over like that," said Noddy,
getting up. "Is your paw better?"

"Wuffy-wuff!" said the dog, and tried to lick
Noddy's face, bumping against him heavily.
Noddy sat down suddenly again.

"Don't *do* that, dog," he said. The dog put a paw on Noddy's knee to show him that it was quite better.

"Oh—I'm glad it's better," said Noddy. "That sailor doll was very very unkind to leave you lying hurt like that. Where's my hanky? Have you brought it back?"

"Wuff-wuff-wuff," said the dog, in rather a sad voice.

"Oh—you've forgotten it, I suppose," said Noddy. "I rather thought you would. Now do go away because I'm cleaning my car. Wait a minute, though —I'll give you a piece of bread-and-butter I didn't eat at breakfast."

"Wuffy-wuff-wuff!" said the dog, and pranced round Noddy in delight.

"It's very difficult to walk with you galloping round me like this," said Noddy, pushing the dog away so that he could open his front door. "Now where did I put that bread-and-butter?"

He found it in his cupboard and held it out to the dog, who snapped it up, and swallowed it all in one gulp. Noddy was quite shocked.

"What a gobble!" he said. "You couldn't even have tasted it!"

The dog ran all round the little house, sniffing everywhere. He even jumped up into Noddy's chair and sat there. "Wuff-wuff!" he said, and looked so pleased that Noddy couldn't help liking him. He went out to finish cleaning his car. The dog was quite useful after a little while—he licked off all the little bits of mud that Noddy had missed.

"Now I'm going out to look for passengers, so you must go home, dog," said Noddy. "I suppose you *have* got a home? Oh dear, now you've jumped

into my car—you mustn't sit in the driver's seat
like that! Get out at once. That's where *I*
sit!"

The dog jumped out and Noddy set off on his
way, singing happily, pleased to see his little
car shining so brightly.

> "Hurry, hurry, little car,
>   Before we've driven very far,
>   Some passengers we'll see,
>   Maybe Jumbo, big and fat,
>   Or Wobbly Man or Fluffy Cat,
>   All calling out for *me*!
>   Parp-parp, look sharp.
>   All calling out for *me*!"

The little car always liked it when Noddy sang one of his funny little songs. It purred along happily, and was very pleased when Noddy had a busy morning.

They took Sally Skittle to school to fetch little Sam Skittle, who had fallen down and hurt his knee. They picked up Mr. George Golly who was a very nice fellow, and gave Noddy two sixpences instead of one, because Noddy sang him a song.

Then Noddy saw Mr. Plod in the middle of the road and felt so lighthearted that he drove the car round and round him, singing him a little song too.

> "I like your helmet, Mr. Plod,
> I like your funny nose,
> And if I peeped inside your boots

> Perhaps I'd like your toes!
> I like your big and boomy voice,
> I like your buttons bright,
> But Mr. Plod, I do not like
> To dream of you at night!"

NODDY DROVE HIS CAR ROUND AND ROUND MR.
PLOD, SINGING HIM A LITTLE SONG TOO.

Gilbert Golly and Master Tubby Bear were nearby and they heard this song, and laughed so loudly that Mr. Plod was angry. "Now then—move along there, move along. Gilbert Golly, if I have any more of your nonsense this morning I'll lock you up!"

Noddy was still driving round and round him and Mr. Plod began to feel giddy. "Now stop this, Noddy—I'm not a roundabout. And don't sing that song any more. I don't think I like it!"

Noddy had a very good day, and made a lot of money. He felt very pleased when he went home, and called over the wall to Mrs. Tubby Bear.

"I've got a lot of money, Mrs. Tubby Bear— listen to it jingling!"

"My word!" said Mrs. Tubby. "You sound rich, Noddy. Now don't go round jingling that money-bag for everyone to hear. There are bad goblins about, you know, and if they hear that you've so much money in your little house, they might come to steal it!"

"Oooh—I wouldn't like *that*," said Noddy. "I'll put it away carefully, Mrs. Tubby. Now I'm going to have my tea. I've bought some new bread and some potted meat and some chocolate cakes. Will you have one of the cakes?"

"No, thank you, little Noddy," said Mrs. Tubby Bear. "I've had my tea."

Well, Noddy put his car away, and then went into his little House-For-One to have his tea. He was very very hungry. He buttered some bread and spread it thickly with potted meat, while his kettle boiled. He set out his chocolate cakes on a dish. There—what a lovely tea—and he had earned it all himself by taking people here and there in his little car!

He was in the middle of his tea when he heard a noise outside. Someone was scrabbling at his door. Then he heard a voice, a very doggy voice.

"Wuff-wuff-wuffy-wuff. WUFF!"

34

5. IN THE MIDDLE OF THE NIGHT

GOODNESS—if it isn't that dog again!" said Noddy. "Well—it will be nice to have a bit of company. Come in, dog!"

He opened the door and the dog bounced in, leaping up at Noddy in delight. Noddy fell down at once, and the dog sprang on him and licked him all over.

"Please DON'T!" said Noddy. "I like having a bath at night, not in the middle of my tea. Stop it, dog!"

The dog smelt the potted meat sandwiches on the table, and the chocolate cakes and ran to sniff at them. He turned and looked at Noddy with his great big eyes.

35

"Wuff," he said, mournfully. "Wuff-wuff."

"Oh—so you're hungry, are you?" said Noddy, getting up. The dog at once leapt at him again and down went poor Noddy.

"Don't do that!" said Noddy, crossly. "You really are a *rough* dog, always bumping into me. If you haven't got a name, I shall call you Bumpy, because you bump me over. Oh, no *please* don't begin licking me again! Look—have a sandwich!"

The dog sat down quietly at once, and took the sandwich from Noddy. He gave it one bite and swallowed it. Then he whined loudly.

"What! *Another* one? Good gracious, what a way to eat," said Noddy and gave Bumpy another piece of bread-and-butter spread with potted meat. Bumpy swallowed that too, and then he snapped a chocolate cake off the dish.

"Why don't you learn

some manners?" said Noddy, shocked. "I've a good mind to put you in the corner for that. Good gracious—there goes *another* of my cakes! Stop it, dog! Go into the corner at once. IN THE CORNER, do you hear?"

Bumpy went to the corner, his tail down, whining. Noddy felt rather sorry for him but he ate the rest of his food very quickly in case Bumpy asked for some more.

Then Noddy cleared away and went to wash up.

When he turned round, there was Bumpy in Noddy's own arm-chair instead of in the corner!

"Get down!" said Noddy, sternly. "*I* want to sit there!"

So Bumpy got down. He ran to Noddy, wuffing,

37

and jumped up at him lovingly. Noddy fell down again, and bumped his head against the table.

"BUMPY! WILL you stop bumping into me and knocking me over?" said Noddy. "You'd better go home. I'm getting a bit tired of you."

Bumpy whined sadly. He waited till Noddy was sitting in his arm-chair and then he ran to him and put his head on his knee and looked up at him so lovingly that Noddy couldn't help loving him back, even though he *was* such a bumpy dog.

"All right—you can stay," said Noddy, and patted the dog's furry head. "You'll be company—but you must go home when I go to bed."

But Bumpy didn't want to go

home, then. As soon as he saw Noddy undressing and putting on his pyjamas, what do you think he did? He sprang right on to Noddy's bed and cuddled down!

"Oh *no*!" said Noddy, very cross. "I will NOT have that. Get off at once—and go home!"

He gave Bumpy a smack and the dog leapt off the bed at once, whining dolefully. Noddy felt sorry, but he certainly was *not* going to have Bumpy sleeping in his bed. He opened the front door and sent him out.

Then he got into bed and blew out his candle. He thought happily of his busy day—and of all the money he had earned. Then he fell asleep.

And do you know, in the very middle of the

night someone came to steal Noddy's money? You see, Noddy had forgotten to lock his door when he had turned Bumpy out—and whoever had come creeping up the path had found the door unlocked—so it could be opened at once. It was easy to slip inside and look very very quietly for Noddy's bag of money.

WHAT a shock for Noddy when he found it gone the next morning! He rushed next door to Mr. Tubby Bear, crying loudly.

"Hoo! Hoo-hoo-hoo! My money was stolen in the night. I think it was a goblin who took it, because there are muddy foot-prints over my floor from the front door to the cupboard where I put my money!"

"Did you leave your front door *unlocked*, then?" said Mr. Tubby Bear, surprised.

"I must have," said poor Noddy. "That dog

Bumpy was with me—and he quite thought he was going to sleep in my bed, so I turned him out. And I forgot to lock the door after him."

"We'll have to tell Mr. Plod," said Mr. Tubby Bear— and soon Mr. Plod was in

SOON MR. PLOD WAS IN NODDY'S HOUSE LOOKING
AT THE MUDDY FOOTPRINTS ON THE FLOOR.

41

Noddy's little house looking at the muddy foot-prints on the floor.

"What a pity you turned out that dog last night," he said to Noddy. "He would have guarded you! Well—it's one of those goblins from the Dark Wood, I'm afraid. It's not much use my going there to hunt for your money—because the thief will have buried it safely somewhere."

"I worked so hard for it!" said Noddy, his head nodding sadly, and tears running down his cheeks.

"Oh, goodness me—here's that dog Bumpy again. Look out, Mr. Plod!"

6. BUMPY ISN'T VERY GOOD

BUMPY came running in at the open door. He saw Mr. Plod and leapt up at him joyfully. Any friend of Noddy's was a friend of his! Mr. Plod almost fell over, but just saved himself in time. His helmet shot off and rolled under Noddy's bed.

Bumpy ran after it at once, bumping into Noddy and sending him flying. Goodness, what a dog! He began to scrabble for Mr. Plod's helmet under the bed. He got it at last, but when Mr. Plod tried to snatch it from him, he began to dodge about here and there, and made the policeman really very angry.

Then Bumpy threw the helmet up into the air and dear me, it came down on Bumpy's own head!

He looked so comical that Noddy laughed and laughed.

But Mr. Plod didn't. What! A dog wearing his precious helmet? What next!

He gave such a bellow that Bumpy was frightened. He ran out of the door, still wearing Mr. Plod's

helmet on his head, very crooked. He dodged into Mr. Tubby Bear's garden.

There he saw Mr. Tubby's rows of seed-labels marking his neat rows of seeds. Aha! Someone had been digging there! Bumpy was sure that Mr. Tubby had buried a bone or two under those labels!

And, before anyone could stop him, there he was, scraping up all the rows of seeds, and sending the labels flying!

Mr. Tubby Bear saw him out of his window. He could hardly believe his eyes. What—a dog wearing Mr. Plod's helmet—digging up all his precious seeds? Mr. Tubby Bear gave a shout and ran out with his walking-stick!

44

"Hey! What do you think you're doing?" he cried and gave the surprised Bumpy a whack with his stick. "Noddy—I will NOT have this dog in my garden! Send him away! And what's he doing wearing Mr. Plod's helmet? Oh, there you are, Mr. Plod! Have you lent this dog your helmet?"

"Of course not. Don't be silly, Mr. Tubby Bear," said Mr. Plod, and snatched his helmet off Bumpy's head. "My word—he's scraped up all your seeds. I'd better take him and lock him up."

"Let me give him a whipping first," said Mr. Tubby Bear, fiercely. But Noddy wouldn't let him.

"No! No, please don't," he said. "He didn't *mean* to be naughty. I expect he thought Mr.

Tubby had buried bones there—not seeds. And you're NOT to lock him up, Mr. Plod!"

"Don't you talk to me like that, Noddy," said Mr. Plod, putting on his helmet again. Bumpy ran gratefully to Noddy and leapt up at him. Noddy fell over and sat down hard on Mr. Tubby's patch of mint.

"Oh *don't*, dog," he said. "Just as I was trying to be kind to you! Look—you MUST go away. Mr. Plod has to find out who stole my money, and you keep getting in the way."

"Wuffy-wuff," said Bumpy, sadly, and backed suddenly into Mr. Tubby.

"*I'm* not helping you to get back your money," said Mr. Plod, in a huff. "Not till you get rid of that dog, anyway."

"All right. But how can I make him go?" asked poor Noddy.

"Get a big bone and carry it—and he'll follow you anywhere," said Mr. Plod. "Take him to the Dark Wood and then give him the bone. He'll

46

bury it there—and stay to guard it. Then you'll be rid of him."

"But I do rather like him," said Noddy. "If only he wasn't such a *bumpy* dog!"

Mr. Plod went off down the road, still looking cross, and Mr. Tubby Bear began to rake over his seed-bed, looking crosser still. Noddy felt rather sad.

"Come on, Bumpy," he said. "We'll get into my car and go to the market and buy you a big bone. It's a good thing I had sixpence left in my pocket—the thief has taken all the rest of my money!"

"Wuff-wuff!" said Bumpy, and wagged his tail so hard that it rapped against Noddy's legs like thick rope. Oh dear—what *could* you do with a dog like that?

7. CLEVER OLD BUMPY!

NODDY went off to the market, with Bumpy sitting beside him in the car. Bumpy was very very proud. Whenever Noddy hooted the horn he barked loudly.

"Please don't bark in my ear like that," said Noddy. "And don't think that the *car* is barking —it isn't. You don't need to bark every time it hoots. Oooh look—there's little Tessie Bear. I'll hoot and make her see me."

"Parp-parp!" said the car. "Wuffy-WUFF!" barked Bumpy, and Tessie Bear looked round in surprise. She ran to the car and patted Bumpy.

"Oh—you've got that dear dog with you. Is his paw better?"

"Yes, quite. But he hasn't been behaving very well, Tessie Bear," said Noddy. "Do you know

48

he knocked off Mr. Plod's helmet and wore it himself? He did look funny. But now he's dug up all Mr. Tubby Bear's seeds, so I've got to buy him a bone and take him to the Dark Wood—and somehow lose him there."

"Shall I come with you?" asked Tessie.

"Oh *yes*," said Noddy. "Bumpy, sit in the back, please. No, DON'T lick Tessie Bear's bonnet off. Oh Tessie, I nearly forgot to tell you. A thief came and stole all my money last night."

"Oh—poor little Noddy!" said Tessie Bear, and gave him a hug. "I *am* sorry. Shall I lend you some?"

"Of course not," said Noddy, and gave her a hug back. "Come along—we'll go to the market and buy a big bone and take it to the Dark Wood."

So away they went to the market, and Tessie got out to buy the bone while Noddy held on to Bumpy to stop him following her. She came back

with the bone neatly wrapped up, and Bumpy nearly went mad, trying to get it. They drove off to the Dark Wood, and when they came to a good place, out they got.

Bumpy leapt up at Noddy in excitement, trying to get the bone, and over went Noddy, bump. "Goodness me—if you were *my* dog, I'd have to sit down all the time to stop you bumping me over," he said. "Here's your bone. Now—go and bury it—and stay and GUARD it!"

Bumpy took the big bone and trotted off with it. He came to a good place under an old tree. He put down the bone and began to dig and scrape, sending the earth flying all over Noddy and Tessie Bear.

And then, dear me, up came a nasty little goblin. When he saw Bumpy digging under a tree, he yelled at him.

"Hey! You bad dog! Stop that!" He ran up to stop him, but Bumpy didn't move. He growled at the goblin—then he jumped at him and knocked him over.

A NASTY LITTLE GOBLIN CAME UP WHEN HE SAW
BUMPY DIGGING UNDER A TREE.

"Tell your dog to stop digging there!" the goblin shouted to Noddy.

"Why should I? The Dark Wood doesn't belong to *you*. He's only burying a bone!" shouted back Noddy.

Bumpy went on digging away—and then little Tessie Bear suddenly pointed at something. "Look —he's digging up something—something buried there! Oh Noddy, I'm sure it's something that nasty little goblin has put there!"

Noddy ran over to see, and the goblin pushed him away. Bumpy at once bit the goblin on the leg and he yelled. "Wuff-wuff-wuff!" barked Bumpy, sounding very angry. He wasn't

going to let anyone push his friend Noddy about!

Noddy saw something deep down in the hole that Bumpy had dug—and he gave such a shout that Tessie Bear jumped in fright.

"It's my bag of money! It is, it is! That bad goblin there stole it last night and buried it here —and he was coming to get it just now—and that's why he was cross because Bumpy was digging just there!"

"Oh—you bad goblin!" said Tessie. "Noddy— he's running away. Catch him!"

But it was Bumpy who caught him and carried him back in his mouth, shaking him as if he was a bundle of rags!

"Oh, you good dog, Bumpy! Oh you CLEVER dog!" cried Noddy, and he gave Bumpy a good

53

hug. "I *am* glad I bought you a bone to bury—we'd
never have found my money if I hadn't! And to
think you chose the very same spot where it was
hidden. Tessie—isn't he clever?"

"He's the cleverest dog in the world," said Tessie,
"and I like him very, very much."

Bumpy so badly wanted to give Tessie Bear a
loving lick for saying that, that he almost dropped the shouting goblin. But not quite. No,
Bumpy felt sure that Noddy would want him to
hold on to that goblin!

"We'll all go back to Toy Village," said Noddy.
"And we'll drop that goblin at the police station.
Mr. Plod will be pleased to see him. Bumpy, you
must run behind the car this time, carrying the
goblin, and Tessie and I will drive very slowly."

And away they went through the Dark Wood,
back to Toy Village. What an excitement!

8. EVERYTHING COMES RIGHT!

EVERYONE in Toy Village was most astonished to see Noddy and Tessie driving slowly down the street, with Bumpy following behind, holding a struggling goblin in his mouth, his tail wagging hard.

"Just look!" cried Miss Fluffy Cat. "Whatever is happening!" Everyone followed the car and Bumpy to the police-station, and Big-Ears, who was just riding by on his bicycle, followed too, most surprised. Whatever was Noddy up to now?

"Hey, Mr. Plod! MR. PLOD! I've brought you the bad goblin who stole my money last night!" shouted Noddy. And out came Mr. Plod at once.

"Ha—there's that dog again!" he said. "Where did he find that goblin? I've been looking for that rascal for a long time! He stole Miss Fluffy Cat's silver tea-spoons last month!"

Bumpy dropped the goblin at Mr. Plod's feet, and then leapt up at him to greet him. Mr. Plod sat down so suddenly that the goblin hadn't time to get out of the way and was almost squashed.

"Will you *stop* doing that, dog?" roared Mr. Plod, his helmet jerked down over his eyes. "Where's that goblin gone? I can't see him."

"You're sitting on him," said Noddy. "And look, Mr. Plod—here's my bag of money! Bumpy found it for me. Isn't he a good dog?"

"No," said Mr. Plod. "He's a dog I'd get tired of very quickly. Take him away. If he jumps up at me ONCE more I'll lock him up with the goblin."

"Oh dear—you'd better come with me, Bumpy," said Noddy, and Bumpy trotted over to him. "No—don't bump me over. Learn a few manners. Oh Big-Ears—this is the dog I tried to tell you about the other day. Bumpy, this is Big-Ears, my very best friend."

"WUFF-WUFF!" said Bumpy in delight and licked Big-Ears on the nose, his tail slapping against Mr. Plod.

"Don't," said Big-Ears and Mr. Plod together.

But Bumpy took no notice. He was very, very pleased with himself.

"Let's go to the cake-shop and have some cakes, and I'll tell you all that's happened, Big-Ears," said Noddy. "You can come too, Bumpy. I'll buy you a big cake for finding my money for me."

Very soon they were all sitting in the little cake-shop, Bumpy very proud to have a chair to himself. His tail wagged so fast that it knocked a cake out of Tessie Bear's hand.

"Bumpy—PLEASE sit on your tail and keep it quiet," said Noddy, and then he told Big-Ears all that had happened. Big-Ears *was* astonished.

"Has Bumpy got a home of his own?" he said.

"No, he hasn't," said Noddy. "I'd like him to live with *me*—but he's so very, very bumpy. I mean—I'd be sitting on the floor most of the time if I had him. And anyway, Mr. Tubby

Bear wouldn't like him living next door, because Bumpy scraped up all his seeds. Couldn't *you* have him, Big-Ears?"

"Of course not," said Big-Ears. "Whatever do you suppose my old cat would say? It's a puzzle, isn't it? I feel that Bumpy has been so good and helpful that he really *ought* to have a home!"

"*I* know!" said Tessie Bear, suddenly. "*I'd* like him. I'm very lonely sometimes when my Auntie Bear is away— and my uncle could easily make him a kennel at the bottom of our garden. I could teach him manners, too—he'd soon be gentle and sweet."

"Well—I don't know about *that*!" said Big-Ears. "But he'd certainly love you and look after you, Tessie Bear. Bumpy—would you like that?"

Bumpy leapt down and ran to Big-Ears. He licked his face so hard that Big-Ears had to get out his hanky to wipe it. Then he licked Noddy and put his head on Tessie Bear's knee.

"Wuff!" he said, in a happy little voice. "Wuffy-wuffy-wuff!"

"*That's* settled then," said Noddy, pleased. "And

Tessie, you can often take him for walks and bring him down to see me, can't you?"

"Oh *yes*!" said Tessie. "We'd both like that. I must go now, Noddy. Come along, Bumpy— and don't you DARE to knock me over!"

Noddy began to sing as they went, and Big-Ears beat time with a tea-spoon.

"Goodbye, dear Bumpy,
    You're clever and good,
    You found all my money
    Away in the wood,
    You'll look after Tessie
    And guard her like gold,
    You'll learn lots of manners,
    And do as you're told!
    You're waggy and licky
    And noisy and rough,
    But I love you, dear Bumpy,
    So, WUFFY-WUFF-WUFF!"

And Bumpy an-swered from away up the street: "Wuffy-wuff! Wuffy-wuff!"

Goodbye, dear Bumpy! Look after little Tessie Bear, won't you?

60